Walter Had
a Best Friend

Written by **Deborah Underwood**

Illustrated by **Sergio Ruzzier**

 Beach Lane Books · New York London Toronto Sydney New Delhi

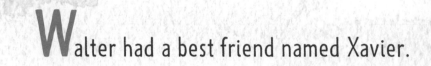

Walter had a best friend named Xavier.

They hiked up the hill together.

They painted pictures together.

They were quiet together.

Walter and Xavier were best friends.

Until . . .

quietly . . .

slowly . . .

they weren't.

Xavier and Penelope invited Walter
to a ball game.

But it wasn't the same.

Walter's world

quietly . . .

slowly . . .

changed.

He didn't hike.

He didn't paint pictures.

He was quiet, but it was sad quiet.

Not best friend quiet.

"I hate Penelope,"
Walter said to his ceiling.
But really, he didn't.

"I hate Xavier,"
Walter said to his mirror.
But really, he didn't.

There was just a big hole in his heart
where Xavier used to be.

It felt like the hole would be there forever.

But then,
one morning
the sun
quietly . . .
slowly . . .
poked its way
through Walter's curtains.

It was a beautiful day.
It would be a good day
for a hike with . . .

It would be a good day
for a hike.

So Walter got dressed,
picked up his hiking stick,
and opened the door.

It was so bright outside
that he squinted.

He started to take
the same old path up the hill,
but . . .

"I'll try a new trail," he said.
The air smelled sweet.
The buttercups bloomed.
A gentle breeze ruffled his fur.

"Nice day for a hike," said a voice behind him.
Walter turned around.

"I heard there's a waterfall up ahead,"
said the badger.

Walter stood still for a moment.
Then he asked, "Shall we try to find it?"

"You bet!" said the badger. "My name's Ollie."

"I'm Walter."

And Walter and Ollie walked up the hill.

Together.

For Kathleen—D. U.

To Cassius—S. R.

BEACH LANE BOOKS
An imprint of Simon & Schuster Children's Publishing Division · 1230 Avenue of the Americas, New York, New York 10020
Text © 2022 by Deborah Underwood · Illustration © 2022 by Sergio Ruzzier · Book design by Lauren Rille © 2022 by Simon & Schuster, Inc.
All rights reserved, including the right of reproduction in whole or in part in any form.
BEACH LANE BOOKS and colophon are trademarks of Simon & Schuster, Inc.
For information about special discounts for bulk purchases, please contact Simon & Schuster Special Sales at 1-866-506-1949 or business@simonandschuster.com.
The Simon & Schuster Speakers Bureau can bring authors to your live event.
For more information or to book an event, contact the Simon & Schuster Speakers Bureau at 1-866-248-3049
or visit our website at www.simonspeakers.com.
The text for this book was set in Argone. · The illustrations for this book were rendered in pen, ink, and watercolor.
Manufactured in China
0622 SCP
First Edition
2 4 6 8 10 9 7 5 3 1
Library of Congress Cataloging-in-Publication Data
Names: Underwood, Deborah, author. | Ruzzier, Sergio, 1966- illustrator.
Title: Walter had a best friend / Deborah Underwood ; illustrated by Sergio Ruzzier.
Description: First edition. | New York : Beach Lane Books, 2022. | Audience: Ages 0–8. | Audience: Grades K–1. | Summary: Walter and Xavier
were best friends until they slowly drifted apart, then Walter meets Ollie which could be the start of a new friendship.
Identifiers: LCCN 2021051971 (print) | LCCN 2021051972 (ebook) | ISBN 9781534477001 (hardcover) | ISBN 9781534477018 (ebook)
Subjects: CYAC: Friendship—Fiction. | Animals—Fiction. | LCGFT: Picture books.
Classification: LCC PZ7.U4193 Wc 2022 (print) | LCC PZ7.U4193 (ebook) | DDC [E]—dc23
LC record available at https://lccn.loc.gov/2021051971
LC ebook record available at https://lccn.loc.gov/2021051972